Jump Up Time

A TRINIDAD CARNIVAL STORY

by Lynn Joseph • *Illustrated by* Linda Saport

CLARION BOOKS/New York

Clarion Books
a Houghton Mifflin Company imprint
215 Park Avenue South, New York, NY 10003
Text copyright © 1998 by Lynn Joseph
Illustrations copyright © 1998 by Linda Saport

The illustrations for this book were executed in pastel on paper.
The text was set in 16/20-point Columbus.

Printed in the USA.

Library of Congress Cataloging-in-Publication Data
Joseph, Lynn.
Jump up time : a Trinidad Carnival story / by Lynn Joseph ; illustrated by Linda Saport.
p.   cm.
Summary: Although she is jealous of all the attention being paid to her older sister's
Carnival costume, Lily helps Christine when she gets nervous before time to go on stage.
ISBN 0-395-65012-7
[1. Carnival—Trinidad and Tobago—Fiction. 2. Sisters—Fiction.
3. Trinidad and Tobago—Fiction.] I. Saport, Linda, ill. II. Title.
PZ7.J77935Ju 1998
[E]—dc21   97-44232
CIP
AC

HOR 10 9 8 7 6 5 4 3 2 1

To my little sister, Christine, with whom I have shared many wonderful adventures. Here at last, you get to be the older sis!
Love,
Lynn

For Etienne.
—L.S.

Is party time, is jump up time.
Oh yeah! Trinidad Carnival here.

Steelband playing in de streets,
All ah we dancing to de beat.
Colors bright and sassy—
Play mas, play mas,
Come and jump with we!

"Mama, isn't that de best song for this year's Carnival?" asks
Lily, dancing around the kitchen to the music coming from the
radio.

Mama only nods her head. Her mouth is full of pins.

"Don't bother Mama now, little Lil," says Lily's sister,
Christine. She is standing on a chair turning this way and that
as Mama drapes shimmery red and green cloth all over her.

Lily frowns. "That old Carnival costume not finish yet?" she
mumbles quiet quiet so no one can hear.

Christine had insisted that since Trinidad was the Land of the Hummingbird, a hummingbird was the only thing she could be for her first Carnival. Who would have thought that one tiny hummingbird would be so much trouble?

Lily shakes her head. For six months, the whole family has been working on this Carnival costume.

At first it was fun. There was cloth to pick out in rainbow colors. There were shiny beads and rhinestones to order. There were hundreds of white feathers to dye in hummingbird colors. Daddy, Christine, and Lily read books about the hummingbird to find out exactly how it looked. Then they created a costume to look just like a real hummingbird.

Lily loves the glitter and feathers all around her. What she doesn't like is how bossy Christine acts just because it's her Carnival costume.

Just then, Mama says, "Lily, please hold up de tail feathers so that I can pin de back of de costume."

"Hummph," Lily scowls, picking up the edges of the tail feathers with the tips of her fingers.

"Stop wiggling it, Lily," Christine snaps. "Mama will get it all crooked."

"I hope she does," Lily mutters, making a face at Christine's back.

When Mama finishes, Christine steps carefully down off the chair and runs to Mama's bedroom to look in the mirror.

"Thanks, Lily," says Mama, picking up the scraps of red and green cloth from the floor.

"I didn't do anything," says Lily, holding open the bag of scraps for Mama.

"Yes, you did." Mama smiles broadly.

Lily smiles a small smile back at Mama.

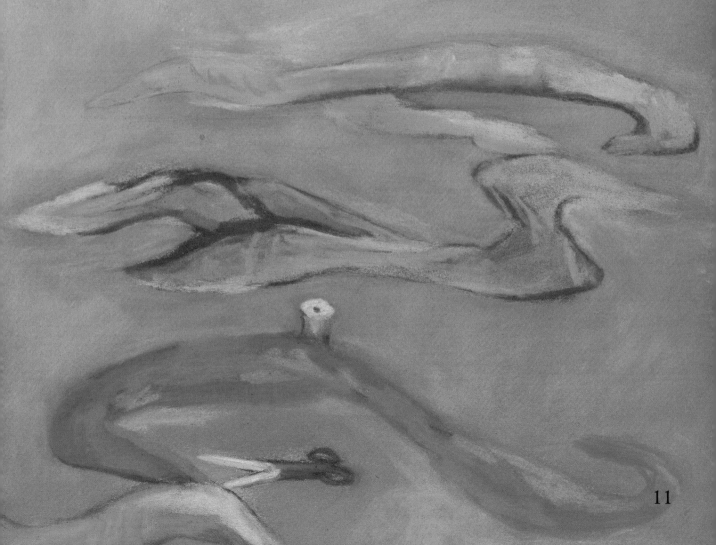

From down the hall, Christine shouts, "Come, Mama, come and see!"

"It go look different in de bedroom?" grumbles Lily, as Mama hurries away.

Lily turns up the radio full blast. But over the beat of the steel drums, she can hear Mama saying, "Christine, you are a perfect hummingbird."

And Christine's squeal of joy, "Mama, I can't wait for Carnival to come!"

"Me either," Lily says to herself. "Because that go be de end of that old Carnival costume."

That night, Mama sits at the kitchen table sewing.

"Come and keep me company, Lil," she says.

Lily watches as Mama sews beads and rhinestones onto the costume. The rhinestones look like bright raindrops landing on a red and green river. The costume is so pretty that Lily can't stand to look at it.

"What's wrong, little Lil?" asks Mama.

"Nothing," Lily grumbles.

Mama puts down the sewing and looks at her.

"You want to play mas, too," Mama says gently.

"Yes, why can't I?" Lily begs.

"You just hold your horses, Lily. When you start school next year, you can wear any costume you want and play mas."

"But next year is too long," wails Lily. "I want to jump up *now*."

"Don't worry, little Lil, we'll have plenty fun watching de bands and costumes." Mama rubs Lily's head.

But Lily doesn't want her head rubbed. And she doesn't want anyone calling her little Lil, either. Most of all, Lily doesn't want to watch Christine dancing all over the house in her Carnival costume.

When Carnival day arrives, everyone is too excited to eat the special breakfast of fried bake and salt fish, even Lily. Daddy can't sit still to drink his coffee. He keeps jumping up to check the stitching and glue on the costume.

"Like he afraid it go fall apart on stage," mumbles Lily. Deep down, she almost wishes it would.

Daddy carries the costume carefully to the car. Mama ties ribbons on the ends of Lily's two long plaits and tucks a pink handkerchief into her sleeve.

"Come on, everybody, we're going to be late," Christine says.

The Savannah is already full of people when they arrive. All
around, Lily sees children putting on their colorful costumes.
There are skirts with bells and sparkles, helmets with spiky
horns, and fat, long tails trailing in the grass.

Lily looks down at her plain brown legs. She wishes hard
that they would turn into something sparkly and special.

"Lily, I need your help with the costume," calls Daddy.

"First, the frame," he says, placing it around Christine. "To
give the costume shape. Now the feathers."

"One yellow layer for the foundation," Mama says.

"One red layer for contrast," Daddy says.

"And one green layer for real birdness," says Lily. She holds
the ribbon up to her waist and swishes the green feathers
around like a pretty skirt.

"Stop!" Christine yells.

Daddy takes the green feathers and puts them around
Christine. "Hummingbirds hum, dearie, not yell," he says
to her.

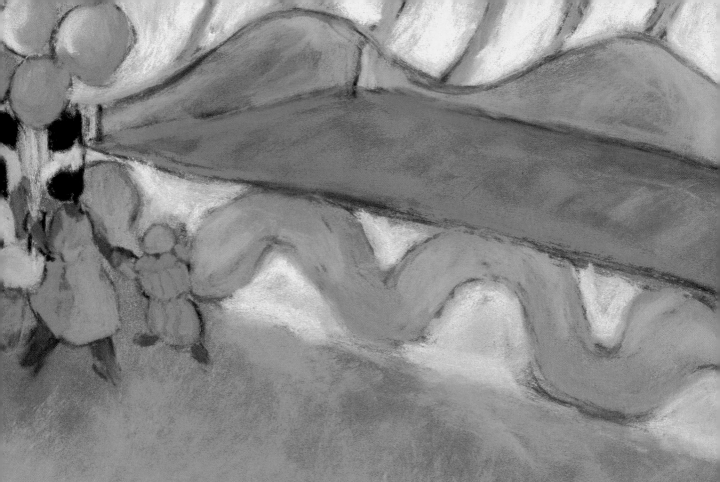

Now, Christine is nothing but feathers. "What a fat bird," says Lily grumpily. But nobody is listening to her. Daddy, Mama, and Christine have turned to look at the soca band going by on the back of a truck.

The band is playing a top Calypso song, and everyone joins in the singing. Lily can't help but tap her foot to the beat. But Christine is standing so still she seems frozen.

"Look at that big stage," she whispers.

Lily looks over at the stage in the middle of the Savannah where the jump-up will be. "You scared or what?" she asks. "Because if you want, I can jump up for you."

"I'm not afraid," says Christine.

The sun shines down hot hot on Lily's head. Mama pours two cups of cold mauby from her cooler. "For my thirsty birds."

Christine pushes her beak to the side to drink. Daddy winks at Lily. "She looks funny," he whispers.

"She looks scared," thinks Lily.

Lily looks again at the stage looming in the distance. The bleachers are crowded with people clapping, singing, and stomping their feet. On the grass, hundreds of children with shiny, painted faces are jumping up.

"If it was me had to go up on that stage right now, I might be scared, too," Lily admits to herself.

She peeks over at Christine. Mama has an arm around her shoulders. Daddy is patting her hand underneath the feathers. To her surprise, Lily sees that her big sister has tears in her eyes.

Without stopping to think, Lily slips the pink handkerchief out from her sleeve and puts it in Christine's hand.

"Is okay, Christine," she whispers. "Just pretend you jumping up in de kitchen at home."

Christine wipes her eyes with the kerchief. "I never jump up in de kitchen, Lily, that's you."

"Well, pretend you're me, then. Jump up for both of us."

Christine gives Lily a shaky smile. "Okay," she says.

Suddenly, they hear music coming from the stage. "It's de Children's Steelband," everyone shouts.

Christine and Lily hold hands tight as the Children's Steelband marches on stage. One boy unfolds a microphone and shouts, "De party now start! Jump up!" And the band rolls into Lily's favorite Calypso.

The Savannah turns into a huge party. All around Lily are giggling tadpoles, laughing poinsettias, and dancing mango trees. A fruit bowl with real guavas, bananas, and pommeracs coming out of his hat is waving a banana standard in the air. An Arawak Indian princess is leading a line of children onto the stage.

Lily squeezes Christine's hand. "Play mas!" she tells her. Christine slips into the crowd to go on stage.

One by one, the costumes go by, in more shapes and colors than Lily has ever seen in her life.

Then Christine's hummingbird comes gliding high above them like a fairytale creature, hardly seeming to touch the stage. The crowd cheers and Mama, Daddy, and Lily clap, whistle, and shout. Lily stomps her feet as hard as she can and waves her arms in the air. And there underneath the beak and all those feathers, Lily sees that Christine is smiling a big Carnival day smile.

When Christine glides down the ramp, Mama, Daddy, and Lily rush over to her.

"You were splendid," says Mama.

"Real bird-i-ful," Daddy jokes.

"De best one!" Lily shouts.

"You think so?" asks Christine.

"Yeah," says Lily, smiling at her.

Then Christine lifts the plume off her head. "Here, Lily," she says, placing it on Lily's head. "It's yours. Thanks for helping with de costume—and everything."

For the first time ever, Lily has nothing to say. She stands still as Christine places the feathers around her and ties the beak in place. Lily is so happy she feels as if she can fly just like the hummingbird.

Mama and Daddy look at her with wide grins on their faces.
Then Daddy starts clapping his hands, and Mama joins in.

"Play mas! Play mas, Lily!" shouts Christine.

And right there in the middle of the Savannah, wearing the
most beautiful Carnival costume ever, Lily jumps up to the steel
band music blaring from the stage.

Is party time, is jump up time.
Oh yeah, Trinidad Carnival here!